Caroline's Summer

Written by Carol Pachik Balog
Illustrated by Briana MacLachlin

First Edition

Biographical Publishing Company
Prospect, Connecticut

Caroline's Summer

First Edition

Published by:

Biographical Publishing Company
95 Sycamore Drive
Prospect, CT 06712-1493

Phone: 203-758-3661   Fax: 253-793-2618
e-mail: biopub@aol.com

Copyright © 2011 by Carol Pachik Balog
Second Printing 2011
Illustrator: Briana MacLachlin

PRINTED IN THE UNITED STATES OF AMERICA

Publisher's Cataloging-in-Publication Data

Balog, Carol Pachik.
Caroline's Summer/ by Carol Pachik Balog.
1st ed.
p. cm.
ISBN 1-929882-60-2 (alk. Paper)
13-Digit ISBN 978-1-929882-60-1
1. Title. 2. Children's Books. 3. Early American history.
Dewey Decimal Classification: 973 American History
Library of Congress Control Number: 2011904548

Dedication

This book is dedicated to Craig. Without Craig's encouragement and suggestion, not one word would have been written. Thank you for everything. You are a good man.

Acknowledgements

I would like to acknowledge my children, grandchildren, and great grandson. Stories have always been a part of our lives.

I also would like to take this opportunity to thank my friends, Debbie and Gloria, for their insight and help-they have provided laughter and support. When I was ready to give up, they were there to say, "You can do this. We'll help." Thank you.

There are references to historical figures and places, but the characters and events of this book are completely fictional. Any references are intended only to give the fiction a sense of reality and authenticity.

I would also like to acknowledge and to thank the following organizations and historical attractions that we have enjoyed:
Hopewell Furnace
Manatawny Park
Pottsgrove Manor
Pottstown Historical Society
Pottstown Regional Public Library
Seven Stars Inn
Valley Forge National Historical Park

I would also like to thank my illustrator, Briana MacLachlin.

Off to the Cousins

"Caroline," Mother called. "Caroline, get down here and let me see that you are dressed properly for your trip to Uncle John and Aunt Ruth's."

Mother was such a fanatic about being "proper." Then again, it was the 1760s and she and Father were proprietors of several stores and sold Uncle John's products. Uncle John was an ironmaster in the Village of Scotts Dam. Mother and Father were leaving the following day for a journey to England. They were going to see my brother and arrange for products to be shipped to the port of Philadelphia for our store: woolen sweaters, material for dress making, fine pottery from Staffordshire, and heaven knows what else. I wasn't much interested in all those things.

I so wanted to slide down the banister, but this frilly old dress prevented me from doing so. I made a "proper" descent. I knew this would please my mother. When she was satisfied that all apparel was in the proper place and everything had been packed, she let me go into the music room to wait for Uncle Ben.

"Uncle Ben will be arriving shortly," she reminded me. "Make sure your bonnet is close by, you know how he hates to be kept waiting."

I amused myself by looking out the window and thinking about Uncle Ben. He was quite a funny man. He made me laugh. He had been friends with Mother and Father since long before I was born. I think he knew them before they had come to America. Sometimes he didn't remind me of an adult at all. He attended all the parties and seemed to be loved by everyone – especially the ladies. He was quite round, and they told me he possessed great knowledge - an inventor they said.

Clip, clop…Clip, clop…I could hear the horses hooves on the cobblestones. I was now getting excited myself. It hardly phased me that I would be away from my parents for months. I had not seen my brother Thomas for a few years. He was much older than I.

Mother had several children in between us, but I understand most of them died quite young. She didn't like to talk about it. I only found out when we visited the cemetery when our neighbor died. Why were parents like that? They never seemed to want me to know anything.

There was a loud knock on the door. In burst Uncle Ben with a great big smile and sparkling eyes. I always wondered, "What is he thinking?"

"So, are we ready for a great adventure?" he asked, as he kissed Mother on the cheek.

"Now, Ben, Caroline is a very proper young lady. There will be no shenanigans. Not from you or anyone else," Mother said.

Our servant carried my luggage to the coach, Mother issued her orders: Must attend Sunday Meetings, must keep up with my studies, must be taught to act and think as a proper lady, must practice the piano, must, must, must. Uncle Ben assured her that Uncle John and Aunt Ruth would be able to take proper care of the "little miss" as they had much practice. Did they not have thirteen children of their own?

Poppa arrived just as we were boarding the carriage for the trip. A hug and a kiss for his little princess, for he was the loving kind. Mother was the strict disciplinarian. Sometimes I wondered how they had ever gotten together.

"Thank you Ben," said Father as he shook Uncle Ben's hand. "We shall get together and I will fill you in with all the news when we return from the Motherland. We shall have a good meal and, perhaps, a bit of fun that evening. I will ask John and Billy to join us."

And then, with Mother's. "Mind your manners, Caroline." the coach pulled away.

Uncle Ben suggested, "It will be quite a long trip. It will get even hotter in this carriage as the sun rises and I think it would be quite all right for you to remove your bonnet."

"But Uncle Ben, Mother would think it not proper."

"Well," he replied, "You are young enough to be able to travel in an enclosed carriage without a bonnet."

I have to admit, I was so happy to remove the bonnet. The ribbons which Mother had tied into a huge bow under my chin were annoying.

We chatted for a while and I decided Uncle Ben was a bit of a dreamer. He talked about having a great hall where all the people could come and read. Books held knowledge he told me. And we should share that with everyone. He also told me he thought we should have a zoo - a place where the children of the city could actually see animals that they had read about.

Sometimes we just sat in silence and watched the scenery go by. Houses were farther and farther apart. It seemed like forever until we reached Mt. Joy. What a marvelous view we had from the top of the hill. I thought I could see farther than I had ever seen before. There was a wonderful field below sprinkled with wildflowers, and I even thought I saw a fawn.

Once we reached Nutt Road, Uncle Ben told the driver to stop at the Inn. We would take our noon meal there. I knew that Nutt Road was the road that had been built by Mr. Nutt the ironmaster to take his products directly to the markets in Philadelphia. It led all the way to Scotts Dam and Hope's Village. Uncle John now owned that furnace, I knew, as I had heard Father talk about it.

The Inn was quite pleasant and much cooler than the carriage.

Uncle Ben seemed to be known all along this route. The innkeeper met us at the door and showed me around as Uncle Ben said this was my first trip. There was a huge well inside. The water was cold and seemed to be all the colder when served in tin cups. There were also enormous fireplaces that served not only to cook the food but also to heat the Inn in the winter. There were rooms upstairs for lodging, and a room that I was not shown. Uncle Ben said that was a room reserved for the gentlemen who chose to have a bit of tonic.

As I peeked in the doorway, I could see a great bar, and a lady. She seemed to be having a fun time with the patrons who occupied the stools. Uncle Ben explained that she was a server. She was not a slave for it was her job. She was paid to serve the guests of the Inn their meals and drinks.

Once the tour was over, Uncle Ben told the innkeeper, "Charles, we shall take our meal at the tables near the creek."

"Fine Mr. Franklin," Charles responded.

The creek was high and swift. I knew it was the creek that fed the well inside the Inn. After a bit of cheese, bread, apples and lemonade, Uncle Ben suggested we sit for just a while before getting back into the carriage. His driver had gone around back to have his noon meal and stood, waiting for Uncle Ben to call for him.

"We will be leaving shortly, Caroline. Let's walk down to the creek and wet our handkerchiefs. We can wipe our faces and lay the handkerchiefs across the back of our necks thereby keeping us just a bit cooler in the carriage." And so we did. The water was so clear I could see the rocks and stones. A fish swam by. It was the best part of the trip so far.

Uncle Ben motioned to his driver. We entered the carriage and we were back on our way momentarily. Whether it was because I had gotten up so early, or whether so full of cheese and bread, I soon fell asleep. It seemed such a short sleep, but when I awoke we were almost to Scotts Dam.

"Perfect timing, Miss Caroline. Once we make this turn you will be able to see your Uncle John's home up on the hill. Now, let's get your bonnet back on you."

Once we turned the corner, I saw it...it was the only thing that registered in my thoughts. There before us was a covered bridge. I had only crossed one once before when Poppa took us to visit the country at Mt. Joy. I was afraid of covered bridges. They were so dark and cold and what if the wood had rotted? We would go falling into the water below and I couldn't swim.

With each sound of the horses' hooves drawing closer to the bridge, I became more uneasy. But, what is a proper lady to do? I held on tight to the edge of my seat and held my breath.

As the sound of the horses' hooves on the road changed, I knew we were entering the unknown darkness of THE BRIDGE.

Uncle Ben spoke, "Miss Caroline, would you do me the honor of holding my hand until we pass over this bridge? My eyes just do not adjust quickly enough to the sudden darkness. I must say, I do appreciate the coolness though. Sometimes, I imagine terrible accidents – another carriage coming the other way, or some such foolishness, like falling into the stream below. It helps me to sometimes close my eyes and think happy thoughts, or to even count how many steps it takes to get to the other side."

"I would be privileged to hold your hand if you are sure it will make you feel better," I said.

I could not believe that Uncle Ben had had such thoughts as I. And, he asked me to hold his hand. I felt very good about that. I relaxed just a bit as I counted. One, two, three......

By the time I counted to fifteen, we were safely across the bridge. I opened my eyes and it was light again. I saw the house up on the hill – a large home, a mansion. It was unlike the homes we had in Philadelphia. It did not have a courtyard, but instead, was surrounded by land. This was going to be quite different than living in the city.

Arrival at the Scotts Dam Mansion

At the top of the hill stood a beautiful, large home made of sandstone and fieldstone. It was surrounded by a grand porch at the first and second story levels. The luscious green lawn stretched endlessly in front. The green broken only by the light of the stone that served as road to the front door. It was a magnificent sight.

There were several other buildings. I could see smoke coming from behind the house and wondered what was burning. There was also a barn behind and off to the left of the smoke. It seemed to be quite large. To the right of the smoke, a smaller home of sandstone and fieldstone had been constructed. It made me wonder who lived there?

Uncle Ben must have sensed my awe and explained, "You shall be able to explore and learn all about country living once you are settled in. I have a feeling you will do and will see things of which you have never even dreamed."

Farther down the hill, the creek that we had just crossed raged on.

I was at once excited and scared. Would I be accepted here and be able to make Mother and Poppa proud of me at the same time? All of a sudden, I missed them terribly. Would my cousins like me? Would I like them? So many questions were running through my mind.

The horses stopped. The door opened, and there to greet us was Aunt Ruth. I was surprised that as mistress of the estate, she wore rather plain clothing. She already had graying hair and wore it pulled back and up in a bun. She did have a smile and that made me feel comfortable as she greeted us with arms outstretched and a quick little hug

She said, "Welcome Caroline. Thank you so much, Ben, for bringing our niece with you. I am sure Anna and Samuel appreciate your kindness too. Come in and let me get you something to drink."

To George, she said, "My man, Andrew, will help you bring Miss Caroline and Ben's things in. After you take the horses to be cared for, you may go to the servants quarters. Jasmine will see to your needs."

"Thank you, Ma'am." George replied as he and Andrew got to work.

Once inside, Aunt Ruth called, "Mary, show Caroline and Ben to their quarters. They can put their things away and get ready for the evening meal." She turned to us and explained she had a few things to finish and would talk with us at the evening get-together.

This surprised me a bit, but not Uncle Ben. He seemed as at home here as in the city. We followed Mary up the stairs to the second floor of the home. Uncle Ben went to the right as Mary and I turned to the left. Up a few more stairs, and the door opened to a huge room.

I was a bit confused as I stood looking at seven beds in one room. Mary said in a quiet voice, "You will be sleeping in the children's room, Miss Caroline. For the summer, you will be sleeping in Miss Rachel's bed as she is at Hope's Village studying the iron business."

She showed me the pitcher with water for washing sitting next to the basin on a little table. A towel hung from the dowel on the side of the table. There was water for drinking and a cup on the table that separated the boys' side of the room from the girls' side of the room. She showed me the closet where my clothes were to be hung and a drawer that I could use. "If you need anything more, please feel free to call for me," Mary told me and then, she was gone. I stood there in amazement. Was she not going to unpack my things?

I turned and went to the top of the stairs. Uncle Ben poked his head out of his room and asked, "Are you unpacked already?" That question made me think that unpacking your own clothes was a normal thing in the country. He told me that since he was only going to be here another day to complete some business, he had packed very lightly. "Would you like a bit of help?" he asked.

I nodded and we turned and went back to the children's bedroom.

I was a bit surprised when we opened my trunk. Inside I found very plain clothes. There were only three very plain dresses. The only frilly dress was the one I had on. School books and paper, pencils, music sheets, and the Bible took up most of the space. There were a few hair ties and pins, brush and comb, and shoes that I had never seen before. Needless to say, our maid had packed my trunk. But, she never would pack what my mother had not wanted her to pack. I was so confused.

There was Uncle Ben with that twinkle in his eye standing and smiling. He reached down, took one of the dresses and hung it up on the hook in the closet. "Everything will be alright. You will find that you have everything you need," he said.

When the things were put away, he suggested I change into one of the dresses and wash up as it would not be long until everyone returned for the evening meal. He went back to his room. I was left wondering what would happen next.

The bell at the back porch was rung, and shortly after, there seemed to be a parade of young people heading for the trough, splashing, laughing, and washing up. Work boots were left outside all neatly lined up along the back porch. Everyone hurried upstairs to change for dinner and it was quiet.

Uncle Ben led me to the formal dining room. It was set with beautiful china and crystal glasses.

I could hardly believe how suddenly different this room appeared - as though someone terribly special was having dinner here. It had to be Uncle Ben. We waited outside the doorway until everyone was ready to enter. Aunt Ruth stood beside us introducing each of my cousins as they entered the dining room.

When the children came to the table, faces scrubbed, hair combed, and manners intact, I could hardly believe these were the same persons I saw at the trough. Some were girls. Yes, I had much to learn.

Uncle Ben seated Aunt Ruth, while the boys held chairs for the girls. I was seated to Uncle Ben's right, and as Uncle John was not here, Uncle Ben served as the head of the table. It was Aunt Ruth who called, "We are ready to be served now, Mary".

Mary left the room and returned with several servants carrying great trays of food. Jefferson carried the tray with fish. Isaac carried the tray with chicken. Mary served the carrots, potatoes, tomatoes and beets. There was homemade bread with butter that melted as we spread it. This truly was a feast.

We chatted as we ate and I learned that the children I would be sharing the bedroom with were named Emily, Jenna Leigh, Julian, Gerald, Michael and Henry. They were the youngest of my cousins, but only Henry was close to my age. Oh no, I had so hoped for a "sister". How would I ever get along with Henry?

At dinner, Emily said, "Welcome to our home, Caroline. I hope you enjoy your stay."

"Thank you," I replied. "It is a lovely place."

Aunt Ruth added, "Emily is my apprentice, so to speak. She is learning this summer how to run the house, how to manage the accounts, and to deal with our slaves and servants. Emily is now fourteen years old. She will most definitely need this knowledge so that she one day will be prepared to run her own household."

Emily was a very pretty girl indeed with big blue eyes, and dark hair. Her hair was braided in one braid and was then pinned up on her head.

Jenna Leigh spoke next. "We are so happy that we will have this chance to get to know you."

"Likewise," I responded. "It is so nice to be able to put faces to people whom I have only known by name."

Jenna Leigh also had blue eyes, but they were a different blue than Emily's. At times they looked even a bit green. I had never thought about colors being the same and different at the same time. Jenna Leigh was twelve years old and she had a passion for the arts.

"Do you often go to the ballet?" she asked. "Have you been to the theatre? I would so love to hear about them."

"Well, not often," I replied. "But I am sure we will have enough to talk about."

"Julian is our student of law," Aunt Ruth said. "You may not see a lot of Julian this summer as he is studying for his exams. He is hoping to join his brother Jonathan in England next year to continue his studies."

Julian responded, "That is true. But having a father who is the magistrate of the region certainly helps make me aware of laws and the process when someone breaks them. I love going to the court and watching father." Julian seemed to be a likable sort, with a sly, shy grin. I was sure he had much knowledge and yet, he was not a braggart. I do think Julian was about fifteen, quite an older man.

Gerald was Emily's twin, I learned. He had laughing blue eyes, seeming to possess a secret - the secret of a happy life. I knew then, that Gerald was fourteen too.

"We will have great times this summer and become friends for life," he announced. Somehow, I didn't doubt his words. . He was so interested in animal husbandry that he spent most of his time working with the animal caretakers.

"Oh, GT!" Emily interjected, "I doubt that Caroline would find your animals a far cry from a great time." Seems Gerald had a nickname.

Michael was the baby of this group. Michael had brown eyes and brown hair. He was quiet and very much into eating his dinner. Aunt Ruth asked him if he had anything to say, and he replied, "I think you are pretty. I think I love you."

Aunt Ruth called, "Mary, please remove our plates and have the ladies in the kitchen prepare our dessert tray."

As we were waiting for the dessert, "I'm Henry," the last child spoke. "I'm nine and I love our farm. I don't think there is anything better than working in the fields. I swear, I can hear the corn grow."

"There will be no swearing in my home Henry," Aunt Ruth scolded.

"Yes, Ma'am," he said. "I love that we can produce almost everything that we need to eat. And animals that can supply milk." Indeed, he did seem so passionate about the farm. He was quite different than the rest, not at all shy, and physically different too. He had red hair that was unruly as it was quite curly, and green eyes.

Desserts of several kinds were put in front of us. So many, I didn't know what to choose. There were apple and cherry pies, and chocolate cake. There was a fruit and nut basket with apples, grapes, strawberries, black raspberries, red raspberries, cherries, walnuts, pecans, and black walnuts. So many goodies! But when Mary brought in the chocolate pudding, indecision was no longer a problem. Chocolate pudding was my favorite.

Uncle Ben nodded to Aunt Ruth. Dinner was a great success. Aunt Ruth dismissed us saying, "Children, you may be excused. Review your studies and don't go too far from the porch. It will be time to settle down and get to bed. The sun rises early this time of the year, and you must do so also."

We got our school books and went out to the porch. The older children sat in the rocking chairs while the younger children sat on the steps. Little Michael found running in the grass much to his liking. It wasn't long until Henry was chasing after him. The next thing you know, Jenna Leigh decided she could run faster than Henry. "I bet you can't," Henry challenged her. The races were on.

Julian chose to be the score keeper.

First, it was Henry and Jenna Leigh. She demanded a head start because she had to run in a dress. She was swift and graceful, and she easily beat Henry. "I'll get you next time. And next time, no head start for you," Henry said.

The races continued until everyone had run. "Okay," Julian said, "Your turn, Caroline." As much as I wanted to run, I had never raced against anyone. "Emily will run against you."

"But Emily has already run and she is fourteen . I'm only eight," I protested.

"That's okay," Julian replied, "We will give you a head start."

I ran as fast as I could, but before I got to the finish line, which was really the grand old oak tree, Emily caught up and passed me. I fell and went rolling down the hill. The children laughed and I felt ashamed and embarrassed. When I came to a stop, I realized they thought rolling was great fun and were rolling down the hill willingly. We climbed to the top, Michael leading the way to resume our seats and picked up our school books. I learned that night, that sometimes people are not laughing at you but, laughing and enjoying their time with you.

Jasmine appeared to let us know it was time for bed. We lined up to tell Aunt Ruth and Uncle Ben good night before climbing the stairs to the bedroom. We washed and hung up our clothes and fell into bed. It was then that I thought of Mother and Father, and here, in a room full of cousins, I felt lonely. But even in the heat, I was so tired it did not take long to fall asleep.

The Raging River

Next morning, I was awakened by the hushed voices of the older boys and girls. They had already washed and dressed and were making their beds. I wondered why were they making their beds when they had servants and slaves to work for them?

It was not long before everyone was up. Jasmine came in to help Michael. She washed his face and helped him dress and then made his bed. She took his hand and led him down the stairs.

GT excused himself, kissing his mother's cheek. "Good morning, Mother. I shall return as soon as the milking is done to have breakfast then."

I was to learn that this happened every morning. Some chores could not wait.

As it was warm, most of the meals were served at the large table outside. We had oatmeal with fruit and large pitchers of milk.

Aunt Ruth asked me to come to her office after breakfast. "I hope you will enjoy your stay with us, Caroline. I realize our lifestyle must be quite different from what you are used to in the city. If you have any questions, please feel free to ask. I will try to answer them, and I will tell you what I expect of you."

"First, I have arranged for Miss Dijon to hold limited classes during the summer as there is a lot of work on a farm in the summer. Second, Mr. Obere will be your music teacher. He will come once a week. In fact, he will be here at four today. Third, our children are expected to learn how to care for themselves. While we have a good life here, they may one day choose to move on and we feel they must be able to do for themselves. Last, we expect them to learn proper manners and ways. All people are treated with respect and dignity. We do have slaves and servants. We will go into details of the difference at a later date. However, we believe all people are equal in God's eyes. Is there anything you would like to ask or know at this time?"

With my mind swimming from all that she had said, I could not think of a thing to ask. "No Ma'am, I can't think of anything right now."

"Very well. You are free to explore the farm today. On Monday, we will discuss where you would like to work first. I thought you would like to try out all the different chores, a week at a time. By the time you go back to the city, you will have much knowledge of the working farm. You may not want to go off alone for the time being. I am sure one of the children will be available to go with you," Aunt Ruth added.

Uncle John arrived and there was a commotion on the porch. After a brief greeting, I headed to the back porch and the buildings I had seen.

"Caroline, Caroline, over here!" Henry called. I headed across the field to where he was hoeing in the cornfield. "Look at this," he said, beaming. "We should have a good crop this year, so long as the weather holds up." He was smiling and sweating as he worked down the row. "I will be done with this row soon and then we can go down to the river."

"Ok. What are we going to do at the river?" I asked.

He looked at me and laughed. "You'll see".

I followed him until we got to the end of the row. When he finished he told Elijah that he would be leaving for the day if that would be alright. Elijah said, "Very well, Master Henry. Have a good time showing Miss Caroline around the farm."

Henry showed me to the large barn. Not only were the farm

tools stored here, but there were also stalls for the animals. Henry looked at me and said, "Don't worry. You will learn, all in good time. We have several barns. This is the largest because the large animals are housed here along with our axes, hoes, and other tools. There is another barn to store our products and food for the animals. And we have two smoke houses. It will all make sense. We grew up on the farm and so it just seems natural to us. I am sure if I were to come to the city, I would have to rely on your knowledge."

"Come on," he said grabbing my hand. "Now, we can have some fun". We passed the outdoor ovens that were so busy yesterday. One of the men was cleaning them. We ran down the hill to the river and followed it to the north. It wasn't long until we could no longer see the house. "This is one of my favorite spots," said Henry. He was taking off his shirt. He sat down and took off his shoes.

"What are you doing, Henry?" I asked.

"Going to check for fish and get in the water and cool off. Aren't you going to come in?" he asked.

"I can't swim," I answered.

"Oh!" he replied. "Well, you could sit on the bank if you choose, and just get your feet wet. Or, we could fish."

I sat on the bank and took my shoes off. I inched closer and closer to the river. The water was cold on my feet at first and felt very good. It was not long and I stood up and walked a littler farther into the water. Henry was having such fun – I envied him.

"What are you doing?" I asked.

"Trying to catch a fish with my hands," he said. "Yuma taught me. He is very good at it."

"Who is Yuma?" I asked.

"He is my Indian friend," he told me. "He is about eleven years old and his name means 'son of the chief'. You may get to meet him one day."

I was getting brave now as I walked about in the water near the bank, but suddenly, I hit a slippery rock and ended up in the water, soaked from head to toe. I didn't hurt myself, and Henry stood there laughing.

As I ventured out farther, Henry yelled, "Caroline, don't. It gets very deep very fast."

Too late, the water was over my head and I didn't know what to do.

"Just kick your feet and move your arms like this," Henry said, demonstrating.

Under the water I went again, and I realized I was being carried downstream.

"Grab a branch!" Henry yelled as he swam after me.

I was sure that I would drown and never see my Mother or Father again. A hand grabbed me by the hair and then, my arm, and pulled me to the bank. As soon as I opened my eyes, I knew the Indian standing next to me had to be Yuma.

Henry arrived momentarily, and he and Yuma laughed. I felt embarrassed and so terribly unattractive in my soggy clothes. Henry said, "Thank you, Yuma."

Yuma just nodded as if to say, "Glad I could help."

Henry introduced us, "Cousin Caroline, I would like you to meet my friend Yuma."

"Pleased to meet you," I replied, tears in my eyes. Of course, since I was so wet, no one could tell they were tears.

"Little fish who cannot swim," Yuma responded as he nodded

again.

"I think maybe we should call her CC - short for Cousin Caroline," Henry said.

"Time we teach her to swim so this doesn't happen again."

We headed back upstream out of sight of the house and I had my second lesson that day. At first I didn't want to go. "But I have music lessons at four this afternoon," I protested.

"Plenty of time," Henry told me.

"Yes," Yuma agreed. "You will learn quickly now. First, you need to take your dress off and let it dry in the sun."

Off came the dress. The two of them must have taught others how to swim. They seemed to have it down to a science. I never felt in danger, as they were close to me at all times. I trusted them. A little while later, Henry announced, "We need to get out of the water and let our clothes dry."

I'd had so much fun in the water, I forgot that my underclothes would give us away if I didn't get them dry too. We sat under the big weeping willow tree and got to know one another a little better.

Yuma knew the river quite well and obviously, he and Henry had a strong friendship. I was happy to be included in their circle. I was warned never to swim alone as the river could change and I should respect its power.

When our clothes were dry, Henry and I went back to the big house. Yuma took his fish and headed north. It was an exciting first adventure. As the summer went on, I became a much better swimmer and was not so much afraid anymore of the raging waters.

We returned in enough time to allow me to practice before Mr. O came to give me my music lessons. He was a kindly old man who had a great interest in religion. He had decided he wanted to be a missionary to help the Indians and told us that he would be leaving the area to go west by the middle of August.

"Thank you for telling us in advance," Aunt Ruth said. "What a noble and wonderful path you have chosen. We certainly wish you well."

I learned much during those several weeks and thought of Mr. O for years after. I received a few letters over the years. One person was kind enough to send me news of his death many, many years later and it made me sad. Yet, I was happy that I had been a part of his life, and he of mine.

Kitchen Duty

Gerald, who was always one of the first children up, woke me quietly on Monday morning. "Caroline," he whispered, "Get up. It's first light and you are to help in the kitchen this week."

I pulled myself out of bed and dressed quickly, though I was not used to this. I almost put my dress on backwards. I washed my face and hands and hurried down the stairs.

By the time I got to the kitchen, Gerald was already out the door and on his way to the barn to milk the cows.

Jasmine seemed too cheerful as she greeted me, "Morning, Miss Caroline. You will be Marie's helper this week. Follow her and do as she says," she instructed as she handed me an apron.

Marie was just a young girl, maybe, twelve or thirteen years old, certainly older than I. "Come," she said, "Our first stop will be the chicken coop. We must collect the eggs for breakfast."

At first, I thought it a bit scary and awkward. What about the chickens? I learned Marie just reached underneath them. Most of them had left their coop when Marie scattered food outside. "Watch out for the rooster," she warned. "He can be very mean sometimes."

"What shall I do with all these eggs?"

Marie laughed as she replied. "I didn't bring a basket this morning, so take the loop at the bottom of you apron and put it over your wrist like a bracelet. Grab the other end of your apron and pull it up. It will make a pouch for you to store the eggs. I am sorry I forgot to grab the basket. I seldom use anything but my apron."

I didn't get near as many eggs as Marie, but I did have several in my apron by the time we finished. We headed for the kitchen, but Marie stopped me from going inside. "We need to wash them first," she instructed as she headed for the trough. "Hurry, but be careful, Isaac and the ladies will be wanting to get these cooking."

"All these eggs?" I asked.

"What they don't use today, they will take to the market to sell. That is, after they allow for the other uses. We bake for the week on Fridays. That is a really busy day."

I learned many things that week: how to crack eggs and scramble them, how to measure flour and sugar for baking, how to double a recipe. It was the first time I realized that arithmetic was an important subject, even in the kitchen. I learned the value of a spring house for keeping things cold. So many things that I had never thought about. At home, Mother and I just made daily trips to the market and country store for what we needed. Now, I knew where the things came from.

While we were busy in the kitchen preparing meals, the men brought in huge containers of milk from the barn. I could not believe that people did this every single day.

Gerald said, "We have to milk the cows, twice a day. What would happen to them if we didn't? And what would we drink or use in our recipes?"

"I don't know," I said.

"The cows would burst their udders," he laughed.

During the week, as I worked side by side with Marie, I learned she was Jasmine's daughter. Mary was her grandmother. They had worked for Uncle John and Aunt Ruth forever. Mary and Andrew had started as slaves, but had earned their freedom. Jasmine was a paid servant. They had a small home in the town that Uncle John hoped to start.

After we cleaned the kitchen after breakfast, I was allowed to work on my studies. Miss Veronica Dijon would arrive at 9:30 am. Classes would last until 1:30 pm and then it would be time to get things ready for the evening meal. Afterwards we would clean up and have a little time for whatever else needed to be done.

Once the week was over, I thought about all the things I had done that I had never done before. I liked shelling the peas. I liked picking the berries. They taught me how to make jam. That was fun. I really was not fond of baking, though, as it was terribly hot when the ovens were lit. But you do what you have to do - if we wanted pies, cakes, bread and biscuits lighting the ovens was necessary. At least the men cleaned the ovens. I have to be honest and say I was not fond of washing the dishes. Actually, I was younger than most in the kitchen, so they had me dry the plates and stack them. Someone taller usually put them away. They also let me set the tables which was a very good job.

Working in the kitchen left many impressions and I learned to appreciate the effort that went into all that had to be done to prepare meals and breads. I remembered these lessons all the days of my life. I wrote them in my journal, along with favorite recipes and accounts of other adventures. One of the best things ever was to be allowed to lick the bowl when we made cakes. Chocolate cake batter was my favorite. We even made ice cream one evening. That was fun, and the ice cream the best I ever had. I wanted to be able to share all these times and experiences of mine with Mother and Father.

Summer School

Miss Veronica Dijon was our teacher. I was quite surprised when I met her. It seemed to me that she would have been more at home in the city than here. She seemed to be quite young for a teacher, but, it was the way she dressed that surprised me.

She pulled her black hair back, but she did not put it up in a bun. Instead, she had long ringlets that cascaded down her back. There was not a bit of gray. She had beautiful very dark brown eyes and a nice smile. While her dresses were not fancy with lace and bows and such, she usually wore lighter colors, sometimes with prints of flowers or polka dots, or gingham skirts and pinafores with plain blouses. It was quite a contrast to our daily wear. Very simple were our dresses, in more somber colors like gray or blue.

She was just as strict and disciplined as my older teacher in the city. She could smile at you and reprimand you all at the same time if you were misbehaving or did not have your schoolwork completed. If you did not have a very good reason, you had better be on time and be prepared for class.

We studied reading, arithmetic, penmanship, and French. The older students also had science and history. History included the European history as well as the history of the colonies. I laughed to myself when she asked Julian how the Commonwealth of Pennsylvania came to be. The answer was that King George had given a grant of land to William Penn for his service to the Crown.

Julian said, "Well, Billy and King George and some other of their friends were playing poker. King George lost to Billy and he gave him the land that became Pennsylvania."

We did call William Penn, Billy, well, at least our fathers did. We children called him Mr. Penn.

Miss Dijon told Julian, "That is not an acceptable answer," but, secretly, we all wondered if it were not true.

I was doing fairly well in French and loved to hear Miss Dijon speak. I could understand it, yet had a bit of trouble repeating what I heard. It was easier for me to write it. Jenna Leigh told me, "You'll get the knack of it. It took me quite a while, but now, I don't even have to think about it. It just comes naturally. It will be that way for you, too, as you get older and more familiar with the language." She was encouraging. I hoped she was right.

One day after several weeks of school, Miss Dijon decided we should go on a hike. Our assignment was to draw something of interest and to write an essay about our drawing.

I decided to draw the willow tree down by the river. Jenna Leigh had seen a family of ducks and decided to do her essay on that. Henry decided he would write about the maple tree and how you could obtain its sap and turn it into syrup. Emily chose to write about the wildflowers and all their uses: could they be eaten, could they be used to make teas or medicine, or whether they were just to be appreciated for their beauty and divine smell. Gerald was not fond of writing, and surprisingly, he did not write about his animals but chose to write about the well on the property. It was Julian's drawing that fascinated me the most. He had drawn a perfect to-scale print of the mansion from all sides. I thought, he was so good he should be a house builder instead of a lawyer.

I added this to my journal, and years later, it reminded me of the secret room and secret adventure that Julian, Henry, and I had shared.

The Secret Room

One afternoon when I had some free time, I decided to write Mother and Father because I was feeling a little sad. I was having a good time and was very busy. I had learned to darn, and quilt, and hoe the rows of vegetables. There was always a school assignment that had to be done and in between, I had found time to have fun with my cousins. But, there were other times when something would remind me of Poppa and Mother and I would miss being at home with them. I climbed the steps to our room, but found I would not be alone after all. Julian was already there. I watched him walk from one end of the room to the other, counting the steps. First, east to west; then, north to south. He would count the steps to the windows; he would count the steps to the fireplace. Next, he would tap on the walls. I thought he was being a little strange.

Finally, I asked him, "Julian, what are you doing?"

"Listen," he answered. He tapped the wall again, walked to the other three and tapped them. "Do you hear the difference?" he asked.

"No," I said. "Do you mind if I sit here and write a letter to my Mother and Father?"

I heard Henry coming up the stairs, "CC," he called, "Are you up here?"

"Yes, Henry. What is it?" I asked.

Once he reached the doorway, he stopped and watched Julian just as I had.

"Ok, Julian, I might have taken a little more space than I should have. But is it really that important to you?" Henry asked.

"What are you talking about, Henry? Come hear and listen closely and tell me if you come to the same conclusion that I have?" Julian said. Julian resumed the pacing and tapping.

I was getting interested in what was going on.

We decided that there was definitely a discrepancy in the dimensions of the room and one of the walls seemed to be hollow sounding.

"What does that mean? Are we going to blow away or crumble in a storm?" I asked with fear in my voice.

You would have thought I was joking. They both laughed. "Heavens no," Julian said. "It means there may be another room on the other side. According to my calculations, it would be about a meter wide. Very small. Like a passageway or maybe a stairwell. That means it could lead to the storage area above our heads. I think I need to study my drawing again. Until we know for sure, we must be sworn to secrecy. Promise me that you will tell absolutely no one," Julian insisted. And so, we spit in our palms and shook hands. "By the way, where did that CC come from?" Julian wanted to know.

"Cousin Caroline is just too long. So, I call her CC." Henry chuckled, a little smile across his face.

"I should have known. Let's go check the rest of the house. It seems to be on this wall to the west. That would be Father's office. Henry and I will check out the wall. We'll let you know what we find out," Julian said as he took charge.

I finished my letter, put it in an envelope, and stuck it in my journal. I knew that I could not mail it. By the time it got to England my parents would be on their way home. I wondered where exactly they were, what they were doing, and if they thought of me. Tears rolled down my cheek and I decided I should just lie on my bed because I didn't want anyone to see me cry.

I heard footsteps, so I closed my eyes and pretended to sleep. It was Jasmine who came into the room. She was busy hanging our clothes on the pegs in the closets. "Miss Caroline," she whispered. "I know exactly how you feel. Once I was separated from my parents, but remember that no matter how far away you are from someone who loves you, you are always in their thoughts." She turned and quietly left the room.

How could she know what I was feeling? Sometimes, older people really surprised me.

Downstairs, Julian and Henry were pleased to find that no one was in their father's office. Aunt Ruth, Emily, and Jenna Leigh had gone to town. Andrew had driven them in the carriage. They were going to see Miss Kayleigh Roth. Miss Roth was a seamstress who had opened her own business in the town. She had a small shop on the main street with her sister Miss Samantha to assist her in her shop. They lived in the small apartment above the store.

Julian had no trouble finding the wall and confirming his suspicions. The question was, how do we get into the space? Perhaps the bookcase was really a door? No, that would be very hard to close after you entered the passageway. There had to be an entrance.

"Master Henry," Isaac called. "You'll do. You don't seem to be very busy. Could you please come and help us in the kitchen, or, are you doing something terribly important?"

"No, just looking for Julian," Henry answered, a slight rise in his voice. "Have you seen him?"

"Not for some time now. I suspect he is still in his room." Isaac replied.

Not knowing what else to do, Henry followed Isaac to the kitchen. *Thanks, Julian, Henry thought. Now I have to set the table and get the trays out for the food. I could be hunting that secret passage way.*

"I'll be right back, Isaac. I forgot something." Henry called as he ran into the office. He picked up a pencil and whispered, "Julian, are you still here?"

"Yes, now go before I get in trouble." Julian said.

Henry took the pencil and went back into the kitchen. He had a little sly grin, but that was nothing new for Henry. Isaac was busy as were the ladies, so Henry got to his chores.

In the office, Julian was busy listening. He had such a keen sense of hearing, he could tell the difference in the sound under his father's desk, and the sound when walking in the rest of the room. He lifted the hook rug and studied the planks under his father's desk. He pressed on the planks but they seemed very sturdy. He hit a knot in the middle plank and a hole appeared. He stuck his fingers in the hole and was able to pull up a trap door just wide enough for a person to enter. He found a string attached to the knot that he had just punched out. He tried to see into the opening but, all he could make out was a crude ladder. He decided if this were the entrance to the passage, one could enter, pull the rug back into place by the way of the string, and be on their way. But to where? For now, he would have to be satisfied. This would take more than one day to figure out.

Julian made sure that no one was around and left his father's office. As he was making his way to the outdoors, Isaac spied him, "Master Julian, Master Henry was looking for you. He is helping us in the kitchen. Would you like to help too?"

Almost made it to the outside, Julian thought. "Yes, I will be glad to help. What would you like me to do?" Julian glanced at Henry with a smile and nodded yes.

"It would be very nice of you to go to the spring house and bring some cool milk up to the house. Thank you for being so helpful. Your mother will be proud of you boys today." Isaac responded.

Julian left, picking up a pitcher to fill with the milk. He was so excited and happy with the secret, he didn't even mind helping today.

By the time the table was set and the trays piled with food, the girls and Aunt Ruth had returned from town and were ready for dinner. The bell had been rung and there was a lot of chatter in the hall as we lined up for dinner. There was quite a lot of chatter at dinner that night. The girls talked about the material they had seen and picked out for new dresses and the patterns they had chosen. There was talk about alterations that Miss Samantha would make. They seemed quite excited.

Aunt Ruth said, "You boys are terribly quiet this evening. Henry, is there something you would like to tell us?"

"No ma'am," Henry gulped. "It was a long day in the fields, is all."

"And Caroline, what have you been up to this day? Is there anything that I should know?"

"Why no, Aunt Ruth. I just wrote in my journal and wrote a letter to my parents."

"We didn't mean to let you out of our trip, but our appointment had been made quite some time ago. You see, Rachel is getting married and these dresses that we are having made are for her wedding. We have to go back in a few weeks, and if you are here, we would love to have you come along." Aunt Ruth said.

"I would be so pleased to come along. Thank you for including me." I answered.

We were excused from the table and were allowed to play. Jenna Leigh, Emily, and Michael stayed on the porch. The girls were still talking about their dresses. Michael was coloring on some paper. I wandered off down towards the old oak tree. I sat on the far side of the tree away from the house. Julian and Henry were off and running. They drifted over to me and Julian told us about the trap door and the crude ladder.

He finished with, "We will need to plan this well, as we will need a lantern. I fear a candle might not do. We certainly don't want anything to catch on fire. That means, we have to figure out when the least amount of people will be in the house and especially, we need to know when Father will be away."

"Do you think we will find a treasure, lots of gold? Maybe some pirates buried it there. Or maybe they killed someone and buried the body there? What do you think?" Henry whispered excitedly.

"I don't want to find anyone's body," I whispered in reply. "But gold would be nice. Or, even some gems."

"We won't know until we are able to enter the secret room. For now, we'll just have to gather what information we can." Julian said. "And stop whispering, the girls and Michael cannot hear us. I do know that Father is going to Virginia next week. He is meeting with Mr. Washington to draw up some maps. So, we get a lantern from the barn. You're always in there Henry. That will be your job."

"What can I do Julian?" I asked. "I want to help."

Julian thought for a moment, "You are often in the kitchen. Do you think you could get a match or two and hide them in your apron?"

And so the plans were made. On the appointed day and appointed hour Julian, Henry and I met in our room. Henry produced the lantern. I reached into my pocket and brought out the matches.

"Good work!" Julian exclaimed. "Today is the perfect day. Mother and the girls have driven back to Hope's Village with Rachel. They are to stop and see Mrs. Bingham and her new baby. Jasmine and Andrew are with them. Father isn't expected back from Virginia for another three days. Father's office has already been cleaned and the rest of the help are busy with their chores. Marie is keeping an eye on Michael. But, we need to be very quiet now."

Julian led the way and we followed him quickly and quietly. He opened the trap door, telling Henry to light the lantern and hand it to him. I followed after Julian, not wanting to lead nor wanting to be the last one either. Henry let the trap door down gently and pulled the string to hide the trap door. Then he put the plug back into the knot hole.

It was quite a large, though narrow, space. It was tall enough for a man to walk through. It took just a little time for our eyes to adjust as we followed the walls. When we got to where the wall should have been, we found steps. We followed them, higher and higher. At the top we found bags. Treasures, we thought. But all we found were clothes.

"Clothes?" Henry exclaimed, so disappointed. "What kind of treasure is clothes?"

"If you have none, and it is winter," Julian told him, "you might be especially happy."

Having not found any gold or pirates booty, I was ready to leave. "How do we get out?" I asked.

"We seem to be at the top of the stairs, so there must be another trap door or something. We just need to test things out." Julian answered.

Julian pushed against the wall and to our surprise, it opened. We were in the small room at the very top of the house. From this side, it appeared that our entrance way was just a small storage closet. We stood there and laughed. All this planning, all this suspense, and all we found was a secret stairway from the office to the top of the house.

"I know there must be a reason for this," Julian stated. "One day, I will asks Father, but it won't be anytime soon. We shall let you know, CC, for I have a feeling I will not ask until I am bound for England. I will write you, if I have to."

A year or so later, when Henry came to Philadelphia with Uncle John, they stopped to visit with my Mother and Father. Henry told me, "Julian said that I should tell you what my Father said when he asked him about the secret room. Father said the man he purchased the home from had had a frightening experience with Indians and some bad mountain men. He vowed that he would never be without an escape route again, and so when he built the house, he had a secret passage built. Father said while he didn't know if he would ever have any use for it, he liked the idea of it being there. He also said that he thought he might use it for a wine cellar."

I laughed as I remembered how Julian, Henry, and I would hide away in the secret room and tell stories. We had used the passage way several times that summer. It always remained our secret meeting place.

The Mountain Man - Paul Michaels

One afternoon Henry and I met up with Yuma at our favorite out-of-sight meeting place: the big old willow along the bank of the river. We decided to play hide and seek. Our willow tree served as our home base. It was our turn to hide, Yuma and me. Henry was It. He turned his back and started to count, "One, two, three, four......"

Yuma turned to me and pointed. He meant that I should go hide in the woods. I ran quickly and looked for a great hiding place. I found a huge rock and crouched behind it. Yuma went farther up the stream. I bet he hid in one of the caves, or he was so good, he could hide underwater. One day he had showed me how.

"Look, little one," he explained. "These reeds are hollow. Pick a long one and place one end in your mouth. Hold it gently, let the other end stick out of the water. You will be able to lie in the water and still have air to breathe."

I had learned to trust Yuma and Henry, so I tried. To my amazement, it did work. Where did all this knowledge come from I wondered, and how come no one ever told me that before?"

Did they teach you that in Indian school?" I asked him.

"No," he laughed, looking at Henry, "Our schools are different than the white man's. We learn the things we need to know from our elders."

All these thoughts ran through my head as I watched to see where Henry would go. My goal was to get back to the base before he could tag me. He passed by the woods, passed by my big rock and was heading in the other direction away from the woods and farther north. I heard a noise. A man on a horse was coming through the woods, and with him a wolf. A wolf. I took off for home, not caring whether or not Henry saw me. I must have screamed though I was so afraid that I didn't realize it. I ran and ran and ran.

Henry turned and yelled, "CC, what's wrong. Where are you going? The base is closer to the river."

I looked over my shoulder and pointed, breathing hard and unable to speak.

"CC, stop! It's okay," Henry called.

The strange man and the wolf came closer and closer. He stopped directly in front of Henry. By then, I had stopped. Not because I wanted to, but because I could simply run no more. Yuma, who had already reached the willow tree came over to where I was.

"It's okay, CC. I understand. He is frightening when you first see him. We call him White Wolfman. He is a large stocky man, dressed so unlike the people you are used to seeing. He has a wolf for a traveling companion. Come talk to him and you will learn that he is just a man. His scars come from life. He is what the people call a mountain man. A person who makes his living by trapping. It is unusual for him to be this far East. I don't know of any rendezvous around here. Come, you will see if you talk to him, he is just a man."

"What is a rendezvous?" I asked as we walked toward Henry and the man. By now, the man had gotten off his horse. He and Henry were chatting.

"A rendezvous is a meeting of the trappers. They sell their pelts and such, and trade for gold coins and supplies. It is strange that he is in this area."

Henry nodded to us. We all walked over to the edge of the

water. The wolf had already satisfied his thirst and was lying in the grass. The man used his cupped hands and drank from the river.

His horse walked in a little way and helped himself, too.

We sat down in the grass as did the man. "This is Paul Michaels, Caroline," Henry said. "Paul, this is my cousin, Caroline. She is staying with us while her parents travel to England."

"Very pleased to meet you, Miss. I am sorry we frightened you. My companion, Wolfie and I have that effect on many people," Paul said.

While his clothes were full of dust and his face was streaked with the grime and sweat of the journey, he spoke softly and very well.

"I thought you would shoot me and feed me to your wolf," I said.

He let out a resounding laugh. Suddenly, I knew that I had nothing to fear from this giant of a man with the long scraggily hair, partly gray, partly black with a scruffy long beard. A man who carried a gun while he rode his horse and had a wolf for a companion.

He rose, and Henry pointed in the direction of the servants house. "Ask for Jasmine," he instructed. "She will know exactly who you should speak to."

"Thank you, Henry. Yuma, it is good to see you again. I'll bet I haven't been this way since you were knee high." He whistled and the wolf obediently got up and followed him as he mounted the horse and rode toward the house.

"Henry, you aren't that much older than I am. If he hasn't been this way since Yuma was knee high, how did you know who he was?" I asked.

"Well, I do talk to my older brothers. Really, CC. I heard the stories. How many people do you know who run around with a wolf?" Henry asked.

Yuma stood. "I must go. I will be away for a while. Be sure to tell her the story, Henry. See you when I get back."

We waved as he turned and headed toward his home. Someday, I will asks him to show me where he lives. Henry and I lay under the willow and he began to tell me the story of Paul Michaels.

"Paul wasn't always old. He was originally from Boston. He is on his way back to see his mother. He had a letter that said his mother was not doing well and she would like to see him."

"Oh my, am I going to get like that too? Old and scarred with dirty clothes? My parents won't even know who I am," I fretted.

"We'll all get old, but I doubt we will follow in Paul's footsteps," Henry said.

"Now, don't interrupt me if you want to know how he got his scars. The story goes that he was up trapping in the mountains. He was not alone, but he got separated from the men while he was checking his traps. As he was returning to the camp, he was attacked by a grizzly bear. The bear almost tore his arm off and supposedly had Paul's head in his mouth. The wolf was there and tried to scare the bear off, but even he was no match for a grizzly."

Henry stood up and struck a pose to remind me of the grizzly-mouth wide open, teeth bared, arms above his head. I laughed, but I understood the picture he was trying to paint with words

"A couple of the men arrived just then, looking for Paul. They shot at the bear and scared him off. Paul was bleeding so badly, they didn't know if he would survive. They tried to stop the bleeding. They put a strip of cloth around his arm and tied it tightly, stopping the flow of blood. They got him back to the camp as quickly as they could. placed him near the river, and cleaned the wounds as best they could. He begged them to sew the wounds shut on his face and arm. They were very unsure of this, so he took the needle and thread and did it himself. That is what caused the scars. He is very lucky to be alive. That is why he looks the way he does. The scars make him look mean and nasty and he scares people."

The dinner bell rang. Henry sprang to his feet, grabbed my hand and said, "Let's go. You know how Mama hates when we are late. She and Father have a thing about wasting people's time and being inconsiderate."

"Race you," I called as I took off.

My dearest daughter, Caroline,

It seems like such a long time since we have departed for England. I miss you already and you can not imagine how happy your Father and I will be to return and see you. I was happy to see Thomas again, but I think this is the last trip I will be making to England. It was not a pleasant trip for me. The sea and I seem to be at odds. It makes my stomach queasy.

The Letter

One week, I was assigned to work in my Aunt Ruth's office with Emily. After breakfast we went to the study and Emily said, "The very first thing we do is check Mother's calendar. It helps us to make our plans, not only for the day but for the entire week. See here, tomorrow she has a note that says, 'Going to town. See Miss Kayleigh and Miss Samantha. Check to see if supplies are ready. Stop to see Mr. Dustin Smithy. Arrange time for horses to be shoed.'"

"What am I to do?" I asked. "I am not sure that I can read all that well. I'm only eight."

"I know. Mother just wants you to realize that even away from the city, we must have knowledge so that we can be responsible. We need to be responsible to our servants and slaves, providing for their pay or their keep. We must be responsible to our business. Mother sees running the house as that. She keeps books recording every purchase and the costs, whether it be 50 pounds of flour or the cost of a slave. She says we girls must be good at arithmetic. It is as important as having good manners."

While Emily worked on things that were too advanced for me, I sat in the corner and darned socks. That I could do. Sometimes Mary would ask me to go to the dining room and help Marie polish the silver.

Today, Emily sent me to take a note to Andrew and let him know that we would need the buckboard tomorrow for the trip to town. As I was passing by the outside fireplaces, I noticed Adam building fires in them. Not far away set big kettles of water. "Good Morning, Adam," I called. "Wow! What are we having for dinner?"

This struck Adam as terribly funny, "I don't know Miss

Caroline."

"How can you not know when you are building the fires and the pots are right there?" I asked.

He laughed again, "Miss Caroline, it's wash day. The pots are filled with water to boil the clothes for washing."

"Oh, I didn't know," I answered. I had never witnessed our clothes being laundered. Just then, Marie came out with a huge bag of lye soap. I wanted to watch, but had to be on my way to deliver the message. I thought I could stop and watch on my way back from the barn.

I found Andrew cleaning the carriage and talking to the horse, Faithful. "Well, good morning young miss. What can I do for you today?" Andrew asked.

"Nothing Andrew, but I have a note for you from Miss Emily. She wants to make sure you know her mother will need the buckboard tomorrow," I said as I handed him the message.

"Thank You, Miss," Andrew said. He stuck the note in his pocket. "I will be ready as will Faithful and the buckboard." I gave Faithful a little pat and turned to go back to the house.

When I passed Marie and Jasmine, they were busy stirring the clothes. As one woman took them out of the pot with a large paddle, the other put other clothes in. The ones that were taken out were put into a smaller wash tub with the lye soap and the slaves rubbed them and used a washboard to clean the clothes. They were then put into clean, cold water, swished around, taken out and hung on the fence. The clothes were left to dry in the sun.

I returned to Aunt Ruth's office. "Message delivered, Emily," I told her.

"Good Caroline. Did you hear the visitor approach while you were out?" Emily asked. "We had a mail delivery from Rachel. They had taken goods to Uncle Ben, and he sent up a letter for you from your parents," she said as she handed me the letter.

I was happy. A letter for me. It made me feel special. As Emily went back to her books, I sat down in the rocking chair and began to read my letter.

My dearest daughter, Caroline,

It seems like such a long time since we have departed for England. I miss you already and you can not imagine how happy your Father and I will be to return and see you. I was happy to see Thomas again, but I think this is the last trip I will make to England. It was not a pleasant trip for me. The sea and I seem to be at odds. It makes my stomach queasy.

By the time you get this letter, we will have been gone a month already, and getting ready to return. Father has been the life of the party in England. But then, he was always more social than I.

I let most of the business to your father, but I have picked out some lovely materials for frocks. And lace and ribbons. We arranged for plenty of heavy sweaters and blankets to be shipped. By now you know that Rachel is going to marry this year and I bought her a lovely set of daily pottery from Staffordshire to start her off. It will be a gift from our family.

Thomas has had so many experiences. I was hoping he would return with us. He hasn't given us an answer yet. I think he is torn, wanting to return but also in love with Europe and traveling in general.

He has been to Paris several times. He paints, you know. I do hope that he has talents that will provide him a living.

Father and I talk of you every day. You are with us always. It will not be long and we will be back to our routines. I can hardly wait. I hope that you are enjoying your time with your cousins and keeping up with your studies. We saw so many things over here. I cannot wait to share them with you. I put the sketches of the new fashions away in my trunk already.

We love you. I would write again, but by the time you would get my letter, you will be on your way home with Uncle Ben.

With much love,

Mother

The letter made me feel good. I hadn't realized so much time had passed already. I did so want to see Mother and Father again, but now I was afraid I would run out of time before I got to see and do some of the things I wanted to do. I folded the letter and stuck it in my pocket until I could put it into my journal book.

Emily asked, "Is everything all right?"

"Everything is fine, Emi," I replied. "Is there anything I can do for you?"

"Not right now." Emily said. "How about I tell you a little about Father's plan to start a town? Then, tomorrow, we will walk around the town."

She continued, "Originally, Father wanted totally square lots, but he had to change that and allow for the river. Both, rivers actually. There are two, you know. One near us, and one that our river dumps into. That river runs east and west. Our river feeds it. Anyway, Father said if you open a business and live in the rooms above or behind it for two years, he would give you the property. Of course, there are certain restrictions. All the houses have to be brick or fieldstone. I'm not sure why. Probably because they will last longer. So far, we have the livery stable, the hotel and restaurant, Miss Kayleigh's dress shop, Miss Dijon's little school house, and so very many churches. Not just the church we go to, but there is the Reformed church, and the other church up the street. Father is trying to get Reverend Muhlenberg to start a Lutheran church in town. We have the country store. Miss Caitlyn, the owner's daughter, started to serve coffee, tea and sweet cakes there. It is a nice treat and we enjoy it. I am hoping Father's plans succeed."

"I am looking forward to tomorrow and seeing the town and meeting the people. Do I need to dress up, or will my daily dress do?" I asked. "I don't want to embarrass Aunt Ruth."

"Your everyday dress will be fine. We would tell you if we had to dress up. The main thing is to be clean, neat, and remember your manners. Please and thank you go a very long way," Emily said.

Trip to Scotts Dam

Aunt Ruth, Emily, and I left the house the next morning to go to town.

"Many times we walk to town," Aunt Ruth explained. "But today we are going to get some supplies and we will need the wagon to transport them. That is why Andrew brought our buckboard instead of the carriage." She climbed up and sat next to Andrew. "Our first stop is at Miss Kayleigh's. I have decided that I would like to send you home with a new dress. That is, if you do not mind, Caroline. It is a gift from me to you."

"No Ma'am, I don't mind at all," I said.

"Good. Then that is settled,"

We were greeted by Miss Samantha. "Good Morning," she said. She showed us to the lightweight cottons, and I chose a rather light blue background with a tiny flower print in white. It reminded me of white daisies against the blue sky. Miss Kayleigh took my measurements and we settled on a very simple pattern.

"Shorten the sleeves, please. Summer is so hot this year," Aunt Ruth told her. "And please, when you and Miss Samantha have finished, will you send it up to our home?"

"Of course, Ma'am. We will be happy to," said Miss Kayleigh.

"Mother," Emily asked, "if we are finished here, may I take Caroline around to show her how the town is coming along?"

"That will be fine, but remember not to spend too much time at one location. I will meet you at the Country Store. From there, we will return home," Aunt Ruth said.

From the dress shop, we walked East on High Street, the main road. Miss Kayleigh's dress shop was the second shop from the corner. On the corner was The Globe Hotel. Emily told me she had never been inside, as they had no need for this establishment. "But," she added, "I hear they have a room off the lobby where they offer hot baths and one of Mr. Stock's sons is a barber so he set up a room on the other side of the lobby and offers shaves and haircuts. For a price, of course. I know the children only slightly, as they attend school up the street at Miss Dijon's school. I suppose as more people inhabit the town, we will have to go there. She will be much too busy to come to our house. But I may be out of school by then. It's just talk some people say."

The livery was across the street from the hotel. "Don't you think that was clever of them to put the livery across the street?" Emily asked. "You can rent a stall for your horse and have him taken care of while you take care of yourself. Mr. Smithy not only feeds and boards the horses, but if need be, he can shoe them too."

I was much too busy looking around to make any comments. Since I came from the city of Philadelphia, I found it hard to get excited about this little village. Yet, I was impressed as most of the people seemed to know one another and were quite friendly.

Next to the livery was the saloon. "I have never been in the saloon either, so I cannot tell you anything about it," said Emily. We crossed the street and stopped to admire some jewelry in the window of the Country Store. Across from the Country Store was the doctor's office with an empty lot next door. Next to the Country Store was Miss Dijon's house and school. It set back from the street, so we could see her yard. There was an iron fence and in the yard was a bell like the one outside Aunt Ruth's that called us to dinner. An old swing hung from the large tree. I thought that I might like to go to this school. Miss Dijon looked up from her flower bed and waved. "Bonjour. Mademoiselles."

After responding, "Bonjour, Mademoiselle, Dijon." I let Emily do the talking. She told Miss Dijon that she was showing me around the town. This was our last stop. We said our good byes, "Au revoir."

I turned to look down the street. "What is down there?" I asked.

"Oh, that building is not completed yet. It will be the jail that will house bad men. I think they are putting the cells in the basement. Father's courtroom is across the street. We must go back and meet Mother now. Are you ready?"

"Yes," I said, although I was still peering down the street. We giggled and laughed all the way back to the store.

"Do you think you will ever have a theater or ballet here," I asked.

"I don't know, but Jenna would love to see that happen. One never knows. I think Father hopes so. He would love to see the town boom. He is such a dreamer sometimes. We do have the rivers here which are a good source for transporting things. We are right on the way to Philadelphia. No telling what will happen tomorrow. We should hurry or Mother will be upset. She hates wasting anything, especially time," Emily said. We quickened our steps, almost to a slow run and reached the Country Store just as the door opened and Aunt Ruth stepped out.

Andrew had brought the buckboard around and helped Aunt Ruth up. Emily and I climbed in the back among the supplies and settled down for the ride back to the house.

When we arrived, Andrew helped Aunt Ruth down at the main door. Emily and I stayed on the wagon until he drove it to the back. Jefferson got on board and went with us to the barn where the supplies were stored.

Once there, Emily and I got down. "I am going back to help

Mother with the accounting," Emily said. "You may go now if you like, to explore or play."

I spent some time watching the men unload the wagon before I saw Julian and GT. I decided I would spend some time with them. Michael was there too. One of the farm dogs was having a litter of puppies. GT was thrilled. I had never seen puppies being born before, so I was amazed.

We would have something new to talk about at dinner, or after dinner. GT said, "Caroline, we would like you to name one of these new puppies. Which one do you want to name? The black one, the black one with the white on its paws, or the runt?"

"Can I think about it a little while? I like them all, you know," I told him. I went off to sit under the willow and think about the perfect name for the puppies, although I hadn't chosen which one I wanted to name yet. I decided I liked the black puppy with the white paws, and I would call him Bootsie. I would tell the boys at dinner. I hoped they would like the name and that he would be a special dog.

Yuma's Home

One day while Henry and I were fishing and swimming with Yuma in the river, I asked if I could see where he lives. Because it was a little way up the river and we would be traveling by canoe, we all had to check with the adults first. I was so pleased that Aunt Ruth and Uncle John allowed us to go and that Yuma was given permission to take us.

We started out very early, just after breakfast. I had never been in a canoe before. Yuma and Henry made me sit in the middle. Yuma sat in the front with a pole, and Henry sat in the back with another pole. I thought, I want one too. But, I had to admit that I really didn't know what to do with it.

Perhaps I would learn by the time the trip was over.

"What kind of a boat is this?" I asked.

"Boat?" Yuma said. "This is a canoe."

"A dugout canoe made from a tree," Henry added.

"Oh," I said. "I have seen lots of boats, even ships at the shipyard in Philadelphia, but I have never seen one like this. How do you make them?"

Yuma explained, "First, we find a tree, that is suitable for our needs. Some are larger than others, depending on how many will be using it. We like to use spruce or birch, but that is not always possible. We shape each end, and then start to dig out the center so that we have room to carry another person or whatever we are transporting. It is a long process, the women and men in charge work several days. They use fire to help burn out the center. Then, they use large rocks heated in the fires. They put notches in the sides in order to make our seats. The canoe is half-filled with water because when the wood gets wet, it stretches. After everything is put in place the water is removed and the canoe left to dry. When it dries, the seats will be secure."

"Are you familiar with many Indian tribes?" Yuma asked.

"No," I answered.

We traveled farther than we had ever gone before. There was a bend in the river and then the village came into sight. I was quite surprised. There were more Indians than I had ever seen. I did not expect there to be so many. I thought only Yuma and his family lived here. There were corn fields planted just like ours, but, the fields were being tended by the women. There were people of all ages. Some of the ladies worked with babies on their backs. I learned that these baby holders were called cradleboards.

"What is that?" I asked, pointing to the round buildings.

"Those are our homes - wigwams. Come, I will show you what they look like inside," Yuma said. "That one over there is ours," he pointed. Inside it was one big room, much like our shared bedroom. I could see the poles that formed the frame for the wigwam. They were covered with woven mats and bark. "We sleep here in the winter and store our things here. We spend much time at the long house."

Yuma showed me around the camp. "Most of the men have gone hunting or fishing. The women tend to most of the needs around the home. Those women are making flour and the women over there," he said as he pointed, "are making moccasins. They will be glad to help you learn."

"This is my mother," Yuma said. "Her name is Dancing Willow." He touched her lightly on the shoulder, pointed to me, and said, "Caroline." Dancing Willow nodded. "She does not speak English as well as she would like to." He turned to his mother and said, "Little fish who can not swim." They laughed and so did Henry and

I as we remembered my first encounter with Yuma.

Later, Yuma and Henry returned from helping the men make bows and arrows to show me how they put the designs on their clothing and moccasins. They were certainly busy people. They wore no shirts in the sun, but their arm bands and headbands were all beaded.

"This is my sister, "Singing Sparrow," Yuma said.

"Hello Caroline," she said.

"Please to meet you." I replied.

"I have been going to the Indian school where they teach us your language," she continued. I knew she sensed my astonishment at her ease in speaking to me. "You may enjoy this job. It is one of my favorites. Are you familiar with our wampum beads?"

"Yes," I said. "We get some of it in our stores."

"They come from shells, the white and the purple. We use some in our bead work and trade the rest for other things. We have to make them. Let's teach you how to put the design on your moccasins," she said.

"My moccasins?" I asked.

"We thought we would give you a pair to take home."

I was quite happy. I slipped them on and imagined what kind of a design I would use.

"Yuma," I asked, "why are so many of the men without hair?"

He replied simply, "It is our way. We either remove all the hair or leave a tuft of hair in the middle. When I reach that age, I will shave my head too."

As the sun moved to the west, Yuma came and told me we had to leave. "I wish I could stay longer, but I know you not only have to take us home, but also return. Thank you. I have so enjoyed my visit and I love my moccasins."

We climbed into the dugout canoe and headed for our end of the river. It seemed all people did the same things, even if they did them in different ways. They worked hard to provide for living, they told stories, and they taught their young.

Yuma left us out of the canoe at our favorite spot by the old willow tree. We waved goodbye as we headed to the house and Yuma set off in his canoe to return home.

Goodbyes and Hellos

"Children, Uncle Ben will be returning to pick up Caroline. We expect him sometime this evening. If you feel your chores will keep you away from breakfast, you may say your goodbyes this evening. And Caroline, you will have no chores tomorrow except to repack your bag and be ready to leave when Uncle Ben is ready. If you need help, I am sure Jasmine or Mary will be glad to help you," Aunt Ruth said at dinner one night.

This came as a shock to me even though I knew that summer was almost over. I was quite quiet that evening. It seemed to have come to an end so quickly. I had all those mixed feelings again: sad to be leaving; happy to return home and be with Mother and Poppa again; sad to think that I would not get to see Yuma. I did have my journal to remind me of all these things.

I went to our room early and started to pack. Slowly, one by one the children gravitated upstairs to help me.

"Would you like some help, Caroline?" Jenna Leigh asked.

"Thank you," I said as I handed her my dresses all except the one from Miss Kayleigh's that I would wear tomorrow. "Do you think my bonnet will look too frilly with my dress?" I asked.

Jenna Leigh stopped folding my dress and went to her drawer. "I have this rather plain light blue bonnet that I would love to give you. Don't you think the blue will match the background in your dress? When you wear it, you can think of me," she said as she handed it to me.

Emily was very quiet as we all worked. "Don't forget your music sheets. I am sure your Mother will want to hear the new pieces that you have learned to play."

"Yes, I am sure she will. Won't she be surprised," I said, "when she recognizes the song?"

Gerald leaned over and whispered, "You know Caroline, I will take very good care of Bootsie. He will be the best herder ever. Border collies have that instinct, you know. But he will be even better than most, I am sure of it."

Little Mikey blurted out, "I don't want you to go. I love you. When will you come back?"

"I really can't answer that, but I love you too," I assured him as I leaned over and kissed his cheek.

Julian added, "I hope you come back soon. I so wanted to show you Father's court room. You didn't even get to see his wig. Perhaps I will be able to visit you when I go to England next year. I will have to come to Philadelphia."

By now, we had packed clothes, books, my moccasins, and all other belongings. Only Henry was missing. I could not understand why he had not come up to say goodbye so there would be no worrying about it in the morning.

We sat on the porch for a little while before bedtime. Still no Henry. Where could he be? When he thought everyone was asleep, he emerged from the hidden room, tiptoed to his bed, and climbed in. Not a word did he say to me. I let him think that I was sleeping. I would tell him good bye tomorrow.

Upon arising all seemed normal. Everyone was getting dressed and going off to breakfast. Uncle Ben was already at the table. GT, was already milking and Henry was nowhere in sight. After breakfast Uncle Ben called, "George, is the carriage loaded?"

"Yes, sir, Mr. Franklin. We are ready whenever you are, sir," George answered.

Uncle Ben turned and addressed Aunt Ruth, "Ruth, your

hospitality is always appreciated. Thank you so much for everything. When might I tell Anne and Samuel to expect you for a visit?"

"We are planning to come to see them in a week. A little time to let them recover from their journey and get back to normal," Aunt Ruth told Uncle Ben. She gave me a hug and said "We enjoyed your stay, Caroline, and I do hope that you have enjoyed being here."

"I certainly have. Thank you for having me," I said.

I climbed aboard the carriage with George's help still looking over my shoulder to see if I could see Henry. Uncle Ben climbed in and we were on our way.

As we were heading down the path to the bridge I heard, "CC! CC!"

I stuck my head out the window to see Henry running so fast from the field, arms waving, with a smile on his face. George pulled the horses to a stop and Henry caught up. "I couldn't let you go without saying goodbye, but that word is so hard to say sometimes," Henry exclaimed out of breath.

"I know," I agreed. "I shall always remember our adventures and you. Thank you so much for a wonderful summer," I answered.

"Until the next time," he said.

I felt the smile spread across my face. We waved until the carriage reached the bridge, and as I reached for Uncle Ben's hand, I told him, "You need not be afraid. The darkness will last only a short while. I will hold your hand." There was a big grin on his face, too, but why, I am not certain.

He replied, "Thank you, Miss Caroline. You certainly have grown quite a lot this summer."

We chatted all the way to Philadelphia. I told him about my

trip to Yuma's village and how I learned to swim. I told him about the town Uncle John wanted to build. I think I even told him about learning to make jam and picking berries. I told him about rolling down the hill my first night there. He seemed to enjoy hearing about my adventures, but of course, I didn't tell him about the secret room.

It seemed to take no time at all until we crossed Mt. Joy and not much longer until we were in territory that was familiar to me.

"I had a wonderful summer. I was a bit sad to leave," I said as the horse was pulled to a stop.

"I am so glad you feel that way," Uncle Ben replied.

The carriage door opened and there was Poppa. He lifted me out and swung me around as he hugged me. "I've missed you my little princess," he whispered.

"I missed you too, Poppa."

Mother was standing at the door with a tall, young man. It was Thomas. My brother had returned with our parents. Now I would not be the only child in the house and there would be someone younger than Mother and Father to talk to.

"Thank you, Ben. Would you care to come in for a bit to eat or drink?" Father asked.

"No, I think I would like to get home myself. I will join you when John and Ruth come next week, if that is all right."

"Perfect, then." Poppa replied.

I greeted Mother and Thomas. "I have so much to tell you," I said as we entered the house. But, of course, no matter how many times we talked, I remained quiet about the secret room.